THE 52-STORY TREEHOUSE

ANDY GRIFFITHS

illustrated by Terry Denton

Feiwel and Friends • New York

A FEIWEL AND FRIENDS BOOK
An Imprint of Macmillan

Our books may be purchased in bulk for promotional, educational, or business
use. Please contact your local bookseller or the Macmillan Corporate and
Premium Sales Department at (800) 221-7945 ext. 5442 or by e-mail at
MacmillanSpecialMarkets@macmillan.com.

Library of Congress Cataloging-in-Publication Data Available
ISBN: 978-1-250-02693-4 (hardcover) / 978-1-250-08023-3 (ebook)

Feiwel and Friends logo designed by Filomena Tuosto

Originally published as *The 52-Storey Treehouse*
in Australia by Pan Macmillan Australia Pty Ltd

First published in the United States by Feiwel and Friends,
an imprint of Macmillan

First U.S. Edition: 2016

10 9 8 7 6 5 4 3 2 1

mackids.com

CONTENTS

CHAPTER 1

THE 52-STORY TREEHOUSE

Hi, my name is Andy.

This is my friend Terry.

We live in a tree.

Well, when I say "tree," I mean treehouse. And when I say "treehouse," I don't just mean any old treehouse—I mean a 52-*story* treehouse!
(It used to be a 39-story treehouse, but we've added another 13 stories.)

So what are you waiting for?
Come on up!

We've added a watermelon-smashing room,

a chainsaw-juggling level,

a make-your-own-pizza parlor,

Pizza dough

a rocket-powered carrot-launcher,

a giant hair dryer that is so strong it practically blasts the hair right off your head,

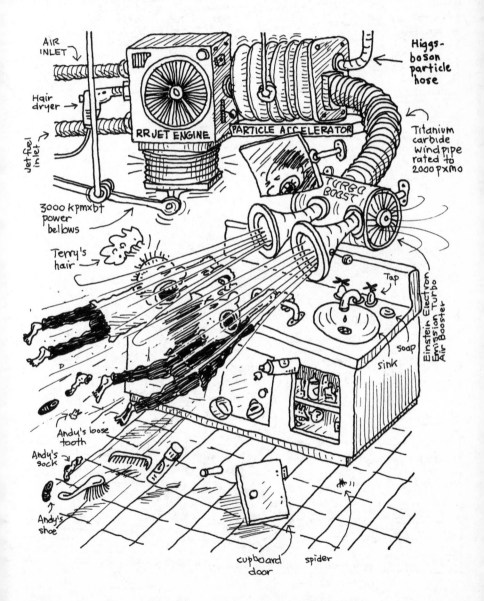

AIR INLET

Higgs-boson particle hose

Hair dryer →

RRJET ENGINE

PARTICLE ACCELERATOR

Titanium carbide windpipe rated to 2000 pxmo

Jet fuel inlet

TURBO BOOST

3000 kpmxbt power bellows

Terry's hair →

Tap

Einstein Electron Emission Turbo Air Booster

soap

sink

Andy's loose tooth

Andy's sock

Andy's shoe

cupboard door

spider

a rocking horse racetrack,

a haunted house,

a wave machine,

a life-size snakes and ladders game—
with *real* ladders and *real* snakes,

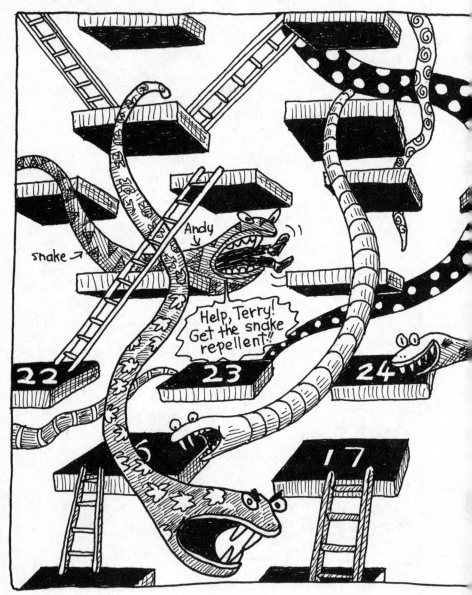

a 24-hours-a-day, 7-days-a-week, nonstop Punch and Judy puppet show,

a remembering booth to help us remember
important stuff we might have forgotten,

a Ninja Snail Training Academy
(Terry's idea, *not* mine),

and a high-tech detective agency, which has all
the latest high-tech detective technology, like a
complete set of magnifying glasses (including one
so small that you need another magnifying glass
to see it), a hot-donut vending machine . . .

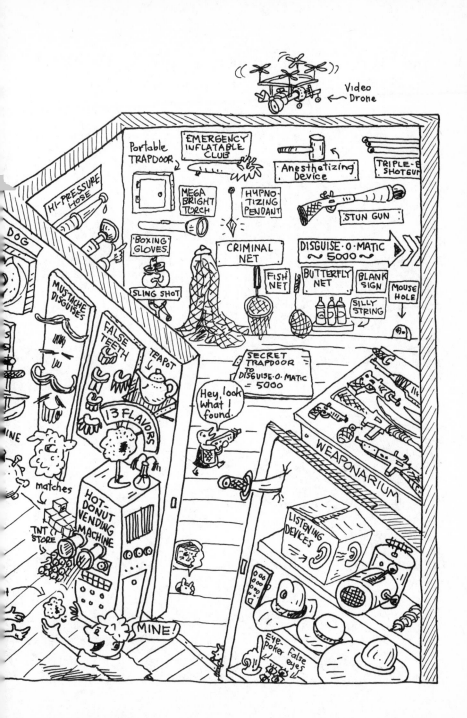

and a Disguise-o-matic 5000, which has a disguise for every occasion!

As well as being our home, the treehouse is also where we make books together. I write the words and Terry draws the pictures.

As you can see, we've been doing this for quite a while now.

Life in the treehouse isn't always easy, of course,

but one thing is for sure . . .

it's never dull!

CHAPTER 2

THE MYSTERY OF THE MISSING MR. BIG NOSE

My birthday

If you're like most of our readers, you're probably wondering how old we are. Well, it's funny you should be wondering that because today is actually my birthday! I can't wait to see what sort of amazing surprise Terry has planned for me.

He's probably in the kitchen baking a cake for me right now.

Hang on . . . I'm *in* the kitchen . . . and there's no cake-baking going on here.

Hmmm. He knows how much I love juggling chainsaws. Maybe he's planning on throwing me a surprise party on the chainsaw-juggling level!

Nope. There are a few chainsaws, a bit of blood and a couple of severed fingers, but no Terry and— even worse—no party!

Perhaps he's planning a make-your-own-pizza party...

I climb up to the make-your-own-pizza parlor, acting like I've got *no* idea that Terry's waiting for me and . . . guess what?

He's *not*!

Okay. I think I know what's going on—I bet he's forgotten all about my birthday and he's in that stupid Ninja Snail Training Academy! He's been spending all his time there lately trying to turn a bunch of dumb snails into Ninjas (which, of course, as everyone knows, is totally *impossible*!).

WHAT SNAILS WOULD LOOK LIKE IF YOU COULD TRAIN THEM TO BE NINJAS.

I climb up to the Ninja Snail Training Academy
and, sure enough, there he is.

"Oh, hi, Andy!" says Terry. "I'm just training my
Ninja Snails. Watch this!"

"Attack!"

"Fly!"

"Use super-Ninja stealth!"

"Launch Ninja Snail death-stars!"

"Start a Ninja decoy fire!"

"Solve a Ninja crossword puzzle!"

"Terry," I say, "they're not *doing* anything."

"Yes, they are," says Terry. "They're just doing it *really* slowly! So slowly you can't see them doing it."

"This is a complete waste of time!" I say. "Especially when there are more important things you could be doing."

"What could be more important than training my snails to be Ninjas?" says Terry.

"Hmmm, let me see," I say. "What about remembering important dates? Like *today*, for example!"

"What's so special about today?" says Terry.

"That's what I want *you* to tell *me*," I say.

Terry thinks for a moment and then says, "Is it underpants-changing day?"

"That's *every* day!" I say.

"Is it underpants-*washing* day?" says Terry.

"NO!"

"Is it Wear Your Underpants On Your Head Day?" says Terry.

"There's no such thing!"

"Yeah, I know," says Terry, chuckling. "But wouldn't it be fun if there was?"

44

"No, it *wouldn't* be 'fun'," I say. "It would be disgusting! I think you'd better go to the remembering booth and remember what day it is."

"What about my Ninja Snails?" says Terry.

"Don't worry about them," I say. "I'm pretty sure they'll be here when you get back . . . probably in *exactly* the same spot."

"Yes, because I'll tell them to stay," says Terry, turning to the snails. "STAY!"

The snails don't move.

"Look at that," he says proudly. "And you said snails couldn't be trained."

We go to the remembering booth.

Terry sits down and I lower the cone of remembrance over his head and lock it into position.

"Okay," I say, "it's ready. You can start remembering now."

Terry gets a dreamy look on his face.

"Remember the time we came to the remembering booth to try to remember what was special about today?" he says, as images of us climbing up to the remembering booth appear on the screens.

"How could I ever forget it?" I say. "Especially since it only happened ONE MINUTE AGO!"

smells
to help
with the
remembering

"Hang on, I'm remembering something else!" says Terry. "Remember the time we set the wave machine to the maximum possible size and had that surfing competition and you got wiped out and I won?"

"No," I say, "I don't remember that at all."

"I'm not surprised," says Terry, "you hit your head pretty hard on those rocks. Look!"

I shake my fist at him. "I'll hit *your* head pretty hard in a minute if you don't start remembering what you're *supposed* to be remembering right now."

Terry continues remembering. "Remember the time one of the ghosts from the haunted house got out and haunted our toilet?" he says.

"Don't remind me," I say. "I was *so* scared, I needed to go to the toilet, but I couldn't go to the toilet because there was a ghost in there!"

"And remember when I put my mouth over the giant hair dryer and my head got really big?" says Terry.

"Are you kidding?" I say. "That was the funniest day *ever*, especially when I popped it with a pin!"

"Andy?" says Terry. "I've just remembered something else."

"Is it to do with me?"

"Yes!"

"Well," I say, "what is it?"

"I seem to remember that I vowed to get revenge on you for popping my head with a pin."

"Never mind that now," I say. "Do you remember anything else about me? *Anything at all?*"

"Yes, I do," says Terry. "And it's quite important too."

"At last! Good work, Terry," I say. "Well?"

"We're supposed to be writing a book," he says. "And it's due any day now."

Uh-oh.

Terry's absolutely right.

We *are* supposed to be writing a book and it *is* due any day now!

"It's strange Mr. Big Nose hasn't called to remind us," I say.

"Yeah," says Terry. "We're already up to page 54 and he usually calls around page 30!"

The 13-Story Treehouse page 33

The 26-Story Treehouse page 30

The 39-Story Treehouse page 32

"Maybe we'd better call *him*," I say, "and remind *him* to call *us* to remind us when our book is due, otherwise we'll *never* get it done in time."

"Good idea," says Terry.

We go to the 3-D video screen and call Mr. Big
Nose. We see his office, but we can't see Mr. Big
Nose. What we can see, though, are overturned
chairs, broken trophies, books all over the floor
and what looks like vegetable leaves everywhere.

"Boy, he sure has a messy office," says Terry.

"That's no *ordinary* mess," I say. "That is what is known in the detective trade as *signs of a struggle*."

"What sort of struggle?" says Terry.

"That's *exactly* what we need to find out," I say.

"Yay!" says Terry. "We've got a mystery to solve! A big one! *The Mystery of the Missing Mr. Big Nose.*"

"We'd better get to our high-tech detective agency and get high-tech detecting immediately!" I say.

"Should I go and get the Ninja Snails?" says Terry.

"No," I say, "they'll just slow us down."

"But they're *Ninjas*!" says Terry.

"They're also *snails*," I say. "Come on, we've got no time to lose."

CHAPTER 3

ANDY & TERRY'S HIGH-TECH DETECTIVE AGENCY

I don't know whether or not you have your own high-tech detective agency, but if you do you'll probably know that it can take a long time to get in because of all the high-tech security. I'm not just talking about boring, old-fashioned big-toe recognition security, either.

I'm talking big-toe, middle-toe, little-toe, whole-foot, lower-leg, upper-leg, left-buttock, right-buttock, lower-back, middle-back, upper-back, chest, arms, neck and head recognition security . . .

not to mention hair analysis,

blood tests,

retinal scans,

a dance contest . . .

and a really hard Andy & Terry trivia quiz!

By the time we finally get in, we're pretty hungry.

"Let's have a donut," says Terry.

"Good idea!" I say. "No detective ever solved a mystery without the help of a hot jam donut."

We eat our donuts and think . . .

and think . . .

and think . . .

and think.

"Well?" I say. "What do you think?"

"I think I'd like another donut," says Terry.

"Me too!" I say.

We get two more hot jam donuts and continue thinking . . .

and thinking . . .

and thinking . . .

and thinking.

"Well?" I say. "What are you thinking?"

"About what?" says Terry.

"About how to solve *The Mystery of the Missing Mr. Big Nose*," I say.

"Beats me." Terry shrugs. "I haven't got a clue."

"That's *it*!" I say. "*You* haven't got a clue. *I* haven't got a clue. *We* haven't got any clues! We can't solve a mystery without *clues*!"

"But where do we get clues from?" says Terry.

"From the scene of the crime, of course!" I say. "We've got to go to Mr. Big Nose's office."

"Great!" says Terry. "Let's ride there on our flying beetroots."

"We can't," I say. "They disappeared about a week ago."

"Another mystery," says Terry, frowning. "*The Mystery of the Missing Flying Beetroots.*"

"Yes," I say, "but we have to solve *The Mystery of the Missing Mr. Big Nose* first. We'll take the flying fried-egg car to his office."

"No problem," says Terry. "I'll just choose a suitable disguise."

"All right," I say, "but make it fast. We don't want the clues to go cold."

"Sure, Andy," says Terry, heading for the Disguise-o-matic 5000.

I'm climbing into the flying fried-egg car when somebody taps me on the shoulder. I turn around. It's an old man.

"Who are you?" I say.

"Don't you recognize your best friend?" chuckles the old man. "It's *me*—Terry! I'm in disguise!"

"*Terry!*" I say. "Quit mucking around. This is serious! Terry? *Terry?*"

He's gone again. In his place is a big, fat, slimy frogpotamus.

Yeuch! I hate those things!

"Get out of here!" I yell. "Didn't you read our last book? The treehouse is a frogpotamus-free zone!"

"Relax," says Terry, stepping out of the frogpotamus costume. "It's just me again."

I step forward to throttle him but I find my hands clutching a metal pole instead of his neck. I look up. It's a stop sign.

"Terry?" I call. "Where are you?"

"Right here," says the stop sign. Terry peels off the costume and laughs. "Gotcha!"

"Stop doing that!" I say.

"Stop what?" he says.

"Stop dressing up like a stop sign and stop playing with the Disguise-o-matic 5000! It's a high-tech detective tool, not a toy!"

"Sorry," he says, "but once you start, it's hard to STOP. Get it?"

"Yes."

"Then why aren't you laughing?"

"Because it's not funny."

"Yes, it is."

"No, it's NOT!"

"Yes, it is."

"STOP saying 'Yes, it is'!" I say. "IT'S NOT FUNNY!"

"Yes, it *is*," Terry insists. "I dressed up like a *stop* sign and you told me to *stop* dressing up like a *stop* sign and—"

"Excuse me, Terry," I say. "I'm very sorry to have to do this."

"What?" he says.

"This," I say, giving him a short sharp tap on the head with a magnifying glass.

"Thanks," says Terry. "I needed that."

"Don't mention it," I say. "That's what friends are for. Come on! To the flying fried-egg car!"

We jump in and pull the yolk down tightly over the top of us.

I press EXTRA SIZZLE on the control panel . . .

and we take off through the concealed flying fried-egg car hatch in the top of the detective agency.

THE DAY WE FLEW OUR FLYING FRIED-EGG CAR TO MR. BIG NOSE'S OFFICE AND NOBODY KNEW IT WAS US BECAUSE THEY ALL JUST THOUGHT IT WAS A FLYING FRIED EGG.

Our flying fried-egg car is the perfect disguise for our undercover high-tech detective work.
None of those dumb animals down there suspect a thing.
Look, up in the sky.
Is it Andy?
Is it Terry?
No, it's just an ordinary boring old everyday flying fried egg. Move along folks, nothing to see here.
BIG NOSE Books
BNB
101
BNB
BNB

We fly through Mr. Big Nose's window and park next to his bookshelf.

Terry takes out the two biggest magnifying glasses and starts looking for clues.

"Hmm, very interesting," he says.
"I see a *magnifying glass* . . .

"I see a *hand* holding a magnifying glass . . .

"I see an *arm* attached to a hand that's holding a magnifying glass . . .

"Hmmm . . . this is a definite clue, Andy, a very definite clue!"

"Yes," I say, "a very definite clue that you are very definitely an *idiot!*"

"Well, I don't see *you* doing any detecting," says Terry, peering at me through the second-biggest magnifying glass.

"Give me that thing," I say, snatching it off him. I scan the office.

There's a book lying on the floor next to Mr. Big Nose's desk. I pick it up and examine it closely.

FUN WITH VEGETABLES

by Vegetable Patty

"What is it?" says Terry.

"It appears to be a book about vegetables."

"Vegetables?" says Terry. "Yuck! I *hate* vegetables!"

"I know," I say. "And so do I. But we have to look at it. It might be a clue."

CHAPTER 4

Dedicated to my darling parents—
squashed but not forgotten.

Hi, Vegetable Patty here. As we all know, vegetable fighting is a serious business, but that doesn't mean it can't be fun. Don't believe me? Well, read my book!

BOIL THEM!

BROIL THEM!

SALT AND OIL THEM!

CRUNCH THEM!

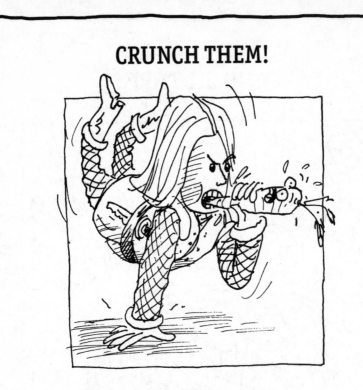

MUNCH THEM!

KNOCKOUT PUNCH THEM!

GRAB THEM!

STAB THEM!

SHISH KEBAB THEM!

THROW THEM!

MOW THEM!

TAE-KWON-DO THEM!

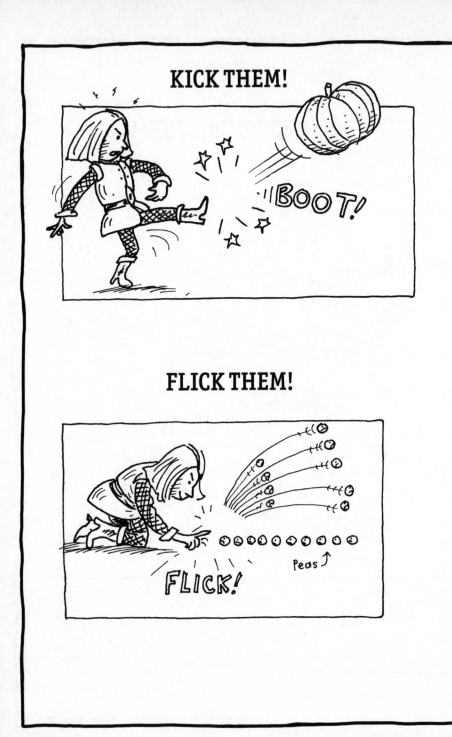

POGO STICK THEM!

MASH THEM!

SMASH THEM!

WHIP AND LASH THEM!

WHACK THEM!

SMACK THEM!

SNAP-LOCK SACK THEM!

CRUSH THEM!

MUSH THEM!

DROWN AND FLUSH THEM!

Brussels sprout on the run.

"That's enough, Andy," says Terry, his hands over his eyes. "I can't take any more. It's too violent! I never thought I'd say this, but I actually feel *sorry* for those poor vegetables . . ."

"Me too," I say. "It's kind of weird to feel sorry for something you hate so much."

"I know," says Terry, "but whoever wrote this book must hate vegetables even more than *we* do."

"You can say that again," I say.

"Whoever wrote this book must hate vegetables even more than we do," he says.

"Terry!" I say. "I didn't mean for you to *actually* say it again, but I'm kind of glad you did."

"Why?"

"Because it's true—whoever wrote this book must hate vegetables even more than we do!"

CHAPTER 5

SLEEPING JILL

"So, do you think the book is a clue?" says Terry. "Does it have something to do with Mr. Big Nose's disappearance?"

"Maybe," I say. "It was published by Mr. Big Nose, but it still doesn't explain where he is. We need to keep looking."

Terry holds up a magnifying glass and continues investigating.

"Look at this pen!" he says. "It's *huge!*"

"And look at this trophy! It's *gigantic*!!

"And look at this paper clip! It's *massive*!!!"

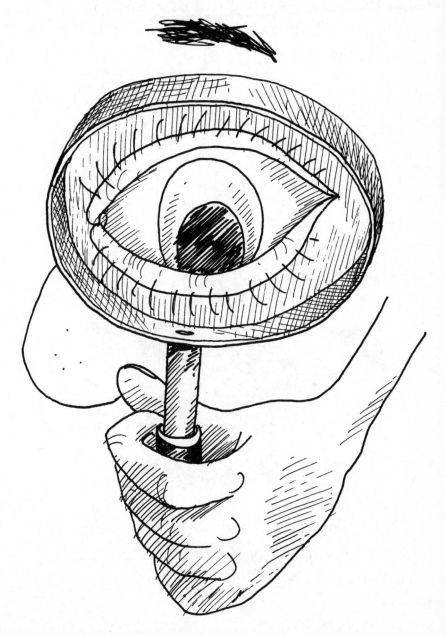

"Um, Terry?" I say.

Terry turns to me, still looking through the magnifying glass. "Yikes!" he says. "*You're* enormous too!"

"No, I'm not," I say, "and neither is that paper clip . . . you're just looking at everything through your biggest magnifying glass!"

"Aha!" says Terry. "Another mystery solved!"

"Yes," I say, "but not the *right* one. We're supposed to be figuring out *The Mystery of the Missing Mr. Big Nose*, not *The Mystery of Why Everything Looks Enormous to You.*"

"Oh yeah," says Terry. "Good point."

Terry peers at a large lettuce leaf on Mr. Big Nose's desk. "Look at this caterpillar," he says. "I think it might be a clue. It's trembling—like it's frightened . . . Whatever happened to Mr. Big Nose, this poor little guy must have seen the whole thing."

"If only caterpillars could talk," I say.

"They can," says Terry. "It's just that we can't understand them."

"If only we knew somebody who *could* understand caterpillars," I say.

"Somebody like Jill," says Terry.

"Somebody *exactly* like Jill," I say.

"Hey, I know!" says Terry. "Why don't we get Jill to talk to the caterpillar?"

"No, I've got a better idea," I say. "Why don't we get the *caterpillar* to talk to *Jill*?"

"But that's the same as my idea," says Terry.

"Sort of," I say, "but mine's better. We've got to get this caterpillar to Jill so it can tell her what happened to Mr. Big Nose so we can find him and remind him to remind us about our deadline so that we can finish this book!"

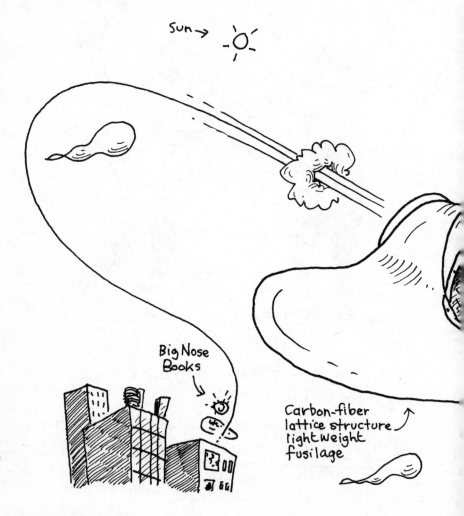

Sun →

Big Nose
Books

Carbon-fiber
lattice structure
lightweight
fusilage

"That sounds complicated," says Terry.

"Not at all," I say. "It's elementary, my dear Denton. To the flying fried-egg car! Up, up and away!"

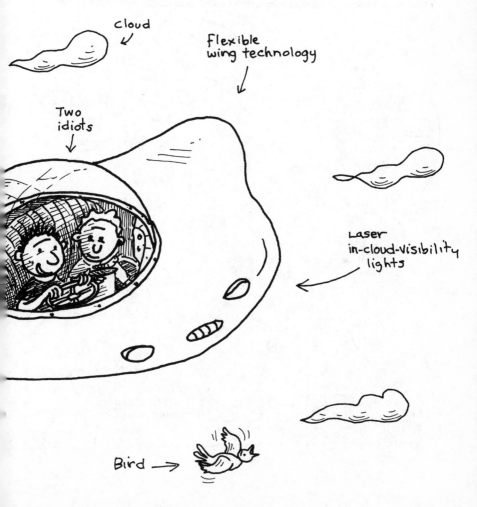

We land outside Jill's house, or at least where we think her house is. It's hard to tell because her garden is very overgrown.

"Wow!" says Terry. "Jill has really let this place go."

"Yes," I say. "I can't even see how we're going to get in."

"I can't even see how she would be able to get *out*," says Terry.

"Maybe she can't," I say. "I mean, have you seen her lately?"

"No," says Terry. "Have you?"

"Not for a while, now that I think about it."

120

"Looks like we have *another* mystery to solve!" I say. "*The Mystery of Why We Haven't Seen Jill Lately.*"

"Yay!" says Terry. "And I've got just what we need to solve it."

He reaches into a bag and pulls out two safari suits and two razor-sharp machetes. He hands me one of each.

"Thanks, Terry!" I say.

"Don't thank me," he says. "Thank the Disguise-o-matic 5000. I grabbed a bag of takeaway before we left."

We put on our safari suits and use our machetes to start hacking into the plants surrounding Jill's house.

We hack . . .

and chop . . .

and cut . . .

and thwack . . .

and hack . . .

until, finally, we find ourselves at the front door.
We ring the doorbell but nobody answers.

So we chop . . .

and cut . . .

and thwack . . .

and hack . . .

until, at last, we smash through the door into Jill's house—and this is what we see . . .

"They're asleep!" I say. "I'm surprised the noise we made chopping and cutting through the door didn't wake them up."

"Yeah," says Terry. "Not to mention the thwacking and hacking."

We go into the kitchen and find Jill. She's fast asleep too!

"Wake up, Jill," I say, shaking her shoulder. "Wake up!"

But she doesn't wake up.

"She's not waking up," says Terry.

"I can SEE that!" I say.

"Shhh, Andy," says Terry. "You'll wake her up!"

"THAT'S EXACTLY WHAT I WANT TO DO!" I yell.

But even my yelling doesn't wake her up.

We try everything we can think of:
megaphones . . .

gongs . . .

air horns . . .

electric guitars . . .

jackhammers . . .

dynamite . . .

but nothing works . . . (Not even poking!)

"Hmmm," I say, "this is no ordinary sleep. This is what's known in the storytelling trade as *enchanted* sleep . . . like in *Sleeping Beauty*."

"Oh, I *love* that story!" says Terry. "But it's scary when the barn catches fire and the horses are all frightened."

"That's *Black Beauty*!" I say. "*Sleeping Beauty* is a fairy tale about a princess with a curse on her who pricks her finger on a very sharp spindle and falls asleep for 100 years."

"But there's nothing that looks like a very sharp spindle here," says Terry, examining the table with a magnifying glass. "Well, nothing except this very sharp carrot."

"Good detecting, Terry!" I say. "Jill must have a curse on her and she pricked her finger on that carrot!"

"But why would Jill have a curse on her?" says Terry.

"I don't know," I say. "Looks like we have *another* mystery to solve."

"Yay!" says Terry. "But poor Jill. Will she have to sleep for 100 years?"

"Not necessarily," I say. "In the fairy tale, Sleeping Beauty is woken by a kiss."

"Yuck!" says Terry. "*I'm* not kissing her!"

"It's okay," I say. "I'll do it."

I lean down,

close my eyes as tight as I can

and put my lips on her cheek.

"It's not working," says Terry. "She's not waking up."

"It might be because I'm not a handsome prince," I say. "It's usually a handsome prince who does the kissing in fairy tales."

HANDSOME PRINCES

PRINCE CHARMING   PRINCE LOVELY   PRINCE DREAMY

NOT-SO-HANDSOME PRINCES

FROG PRINCE   PRINCE NOT-SO-CHARMING   PRINCE POTATO

"Well, I guess we need a handsome prince then," says Terry. "But where will we find one of those?"

"What about that castle?" I say.

"What castle?" says Terry.

"*That* castle!" I say, pointing to a castle on a distant hill just visible through Jill's overgrown window.

"Oh, *that* castle," says Terry. "Funny, but I've never noticed it before."

"Me neither," I say, "but it sure looks like the sort of castle where you'd find a handsome prince. Grab Jill, put her in a glass coffin, get the caterpillar and let's go!"

"Um, Andy," says Terry. "There's one small problem."
"What's that?" I say.

"The caterpillar has eaten our flying fried-egg car!"

CHAPTER 6

JOURNEY TO THE CASTLE

"Well, that's just *great*," I say, looking at the remains of our flying fried-egg car. "How are we supposed to get to the castle now?"

"Don't worry," says Terry. "I've got just the thing!"

He reaches into his bag and pulls out a horse costume.

"How is that going to help us get to the castle?" I say.

"Simple," says Terry. "You put it on and I'll ride you there."

Terry hands me the costume.

"Nuh-uh," I say, handing it back. "How about *you* put it on and I ride *you* there!"

"I've got a better idea," says Terry, passing the costume back to me. "How about we take turns?"

"GREAT idea," I say. "And since you thought of it, you can go first."

"Thanks, Andy!" says Terry, taking the costume. "You're a real pal."

He puts it on and we set off.

"What a lovely day for horse-riding," I say.

"Is it your turn to be the horse yet?" says Terry.

"No, not yet," I say.

"How's the caterpillar?" says Terry.

"Good," I say. "I think it's really enjoying the ride."

"I sure hope we don't come across anything that would be hazardous to caterpillars on our journey," says Terry.

"Me too," I say, as an enormous
black bird swoops down
toward us.

"Are birds hazardous to
caterpillars?" says Terry.

"Yes!" I say.

I reach out to put my hand over the caterpillar but
before I can cover it the caterpillar rears up . . .

opens its
mouth . . .

and swallows
the bird in one
gulp!

SNAP!

"What happened?" says Terry. "Is the caterpillar okay?"

"It's fine," I say. "But that bird's not doing so well. The caterpillar just ate it."

"I never thought a caterpillar could eat a bird!" says Terry.

"Neither did I," I say. "It must be a bird-eating caterpillar."

We continue along the road and come to a sharp bend. We hear a loud, rumbling noise.

"What do you think that is?" says Terry.

"I may be wrong—and I hope I am," I say, "but it sounds like two steamrollers having a race."

"You're right!" says Terry, as two steamrollers come speeding around the bend toward us!

"Start galloping," I say to Terry, "as fast as you can!"

Terry looks around frantically. "I can't gallop," he says. "I'm not a real horse, you know!"

"Then we're doomed!" I say. "If the first steamroller doesn't squash us flat, the second one will for sure!"

At that moment, the caterpillar jumps off Terry's head, leaps down onto the road and starts inching its way toward the steamrollers.

"NOOOOO!" says Terry, putting his hooves over his eyes.

I can't bear to look either. I turn away and prepare myself for the sound of a caterpillar being squashed by two speeding steamrollers . . . but instead I hear the sound of a caterpillar burping.

I look up.

The steamrollers are nowhere to be seen and the caterpillar is licking its tiny little lips.

"I don't believe it!" I say. "It ate two speeding steamrollers!"

"That caterpillar saved our lives!" says Terry.

"That's weird," I say. "I can smell rhinoceroses."

"Yeah, me too," says Terry. "And I can *see* them. Three big ones—charging right at us!"

But before we even have time to panic the caterpillar rears up and opens its mouth wide.

"Wow! I've never seen a caterpillar eat three charging rhinoceroses before!" says Terry.

"What about four wacky waving inflatable arm-flailing tube men?" I say.

"Nope, I haven't seen that either," says Terry. "Why do you ask?"

"Because there's four of them blocking the road ahead."

"Cool!" says Terry. "I *love* those guys!"

"So does the caterpillar," I say. "Look at it go!"

"Those poor wacky waving inflatable arm-flailing tube men," says Terry. "They didn't deserve to die like that."

"What about those five giant mutant spiders?" I say.

"They definitely deserve to die like that," says Terry. "GO LITTLE CATERPILLAR, GO!"

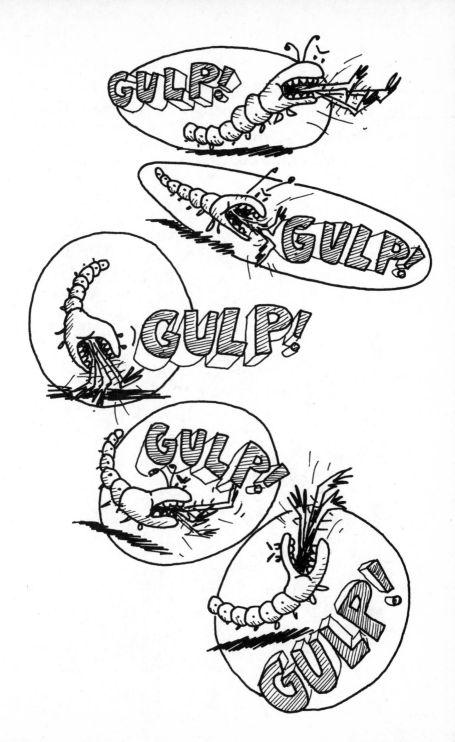

"It's lucky we brought this caterpillar with us," says Terry. "This is the most dangerous road ever! There ought to be a warning sign."

"There is," I say. "Look!"

WARNING!
ENORMOUS BIRDS,
SPEEDING STEAMROLLERS,
CHARGING RHINOCEROSES,
WACKY WAVING INFLATABLE
ARM-FLAILING TUBEMEN
& GIANT MUTANT SPIDERS
USE THIS ROAD...
SO
WATCH
OUT!!!

We walk on. "I'm tired," says Terry. "Is it your turn to be the horse yet?"

"Not yet," I say. "Besides, we're almost there. Look!"

On the hill ahead of us is the castle. It's surrounded by a wall of asparagus spears.

"Gee, they've really gone with the vegetable theme, haven't they?" says Terry.

"That's because it's a *vegetable* castle," says a wrinkled old tomato sitting by the side of the road.

"A *vegetable* castle?" I say.

"Yes, it sprouted a few days ago," says the tomato. "It's part of Prince Potato's Vegetable Kingdom."

"Great!" I say. "We need a prince to wake our friend here from her enchanted sleep. Giddy-up, Terry!"

"Not so fast," says the tomato, blocking our way. "You can't go up *there*. You shouldn't even be *here*. The castle and its surroundings are for vegetables only!"

"Then what are *you* doing here?" I say. "*You're* not a vegetable. You're a fruit."

"I am *so* a vegetable," says the tomato. "When was the last time you ate a *tomato* for dessert? You have *fruit* for dessert. Tomatoes are strictly *main course*!"

"But you have seeds and you grow from the flowering part of a plant," says Terry, "which *technically* makes you a *fruit*."

"You want to get technical?" says the tomato, growing quite red in the face. "Well, let me tell you, Buddy, that no less an authority than the United States Supreme Court has ruled that a tomato is a vegetable for the purposes of customs regulations, *so there*."

"Okay, okay," I say, trying to calm it down. "If you say you're a vegetable, then you're a vegetable— even if you *do* have seeds . . ."

"Don't talk to me about *seeds*," spits the tomato. "*Cucumbers* have seeds and you never hear anybody calling them a fruit. And peppers have *hundreds* of seeds, but nobody would mistake one of them for a fruit! And what about squash? Seeds! Seeds all the way through! And don't even get me started on rutabagas . . ."

"What *is* a rutabaga?" whispers Terry.

"I don't know," I say. "But I get the feeling we're about to find out."

Terry sighs. "We're *never* going to get to that castle."

"Shhh!" I say. "Listen!"

"I can't hear anything."

"That's my point," I say. "The tomato has stopped talking."

"There's a reason for that," says Terry. "The caterpillar just ate it."

"That's the first healthy choice it's made all day," I say.

CHAPTER 7

THE VEGETABLE KINGDOM

We start climbing the hill toward the castle.

We ignore all the warning signs and continue climbing until we come to the wall of asparagus spears. It's thicker and higher than it looked from the bottom of the hill.

"There's no way we're going to get through that!" says Terry. "Not in a million years! Not in a trillion years! Not in a *million trillion gazillion*—"

"Terry!" I say.

"What?"

"Come on! The caterpillar's eaten a hole through the wall!"

"That was a lot quicker than I thought," says Terry. "I must have made a mistake in my calculations. Let me just check where I went wrong . . ."

"It doesn't matter," I say. "Keep moving!"

We follow the caterpillar into the tunnel.

We arrive at the end of the tunnel and peek out.
It's horrible. There's a garden full of vegetables!

181

"We can't go out there," says Terry. "We're not vegetables."

"Good point," I say. "Do you have any vegetable disguises in your takeaway bag?"

Terry looks through his bag. "I've got three," he says.

"Perfect," I say. "That's the exact amount we need!"

I choose the corn on a cob, give Terry the broccoli, and we put the carrot on Jill.

As we enter the garden a trumpet sounds and we see a group of official-looking vegetables making their way toward us.

"All hail, Prince Potato," says a bugle-blowing eggplant.

"That must be him! That's Prince Potato!" says
Terry, pointing to a large potato wearing a small
golden crown. "But he's not very handsome."

"No," I say. "He's pretty good-looking for a
potato though."

"Oh, my!" says the prince, stopping next to us. "Do my ten eyes deceive or is this a princess in a glass coffin I see before me?"

"No," says Terry, "Jill's not a—"

I stamp on Terry's foot to shut him up.

"Yes, Your Highness!" I say quickly. "She is indeed a princess but she is under a terrible spell and only the kiss of a handsome prince will wake her."

"Oh, how beautiful she is!" says the prince. "Her skin is more orange than the sun, her hair greener than grass and her face sweeter than the sweetest pea of summer. I must kiss her immediately and marry her before the day is through!"

"Um, Andy," whispers Terry, "I don't think Jill's going to want to marry a potato."

"Shhh," I say, "we'll worry about that later . . . after he's woken her up."

Prince Potato leans down and kisses Jill.
Quite loudly.

Jill blinks, opens her eyes, looks up at the prince
. . . and screams. (Also quite loudly.)

The prince, startled, falls backward and lies on the ground, his arms and legs wriggling helplessly.

Jill stands up and looks down at him. "Did you just *kiss* me?" she says.

"Yes, my fair carrot princess," he says. "I woke you from your enchanted slumber and now we can marry and live happily ever after."

"I don't know who you are or what you're talking about," says Jill, "but I *do* know that I'm *not* a carrot. Or a princess, for that matter."

She starts tugging at the top of her carrot costume. "And what is this stupid thing on my head?"

"No!" I say, lunging toward her, but it's too late.

She pulls off her carrot head and the vegetables scream.

"That princess is no carrot!" shouts an eggplant. "She's a human being!"

"Seize her!" says the prince.

"Uh-oh," I say, grabbing Jill's hand. "We'd better get out of here. Come with us."

"What's going on?" says Jill. "Who are you?"

"It's *me*—Andy! And that piece of broccoli is Terry."

"Hi, Jill!" says Terry.

"Is this a dream?" says Jill.

"Not really," I say. "It's more like a nightmare. I'll explain later. Run!"

We try to head back through the tunnel but the entrance is blocked by a big, ugly pumpkin.

We turn back and are bombarded by a brutal battalion of brussels sprouts.

We run across the courtyard to a set of stairs only to be repelled by a reeking gang of ginger, garlic and onions.

We are trying to decide where to run next, when millions of mushrooms emerge out of the ground and surround us.

"Take those villainous vegetable-impersonators to the dungeon," says the prince. "I'll deal with them later."

The mushrooms tie us up and drag us down a long cold corridor . . .

open a heavily reinforced celery door . . .

and throw us into a small dark dungeon.

"Well, that all worked out pretty well," says Terry.

"How do you figure that?" I say.

"Well, Jill's awake now," he says. "That's what we came here for, isn't it?"

"Ye-es," I say, "that was *part* of it. But we also wanted her to talk to the caterpillar so we could find out what happened to Mr. Big Nose."

"You don't need a caterpillar for that," booms a familiar voice. "I can tell you myself. I'm right here!"

CHAPTER 8

THE DUNGEON

"Mr. Big Nose?!" says Terry. "Is that *you*?"

"Of course it's me!" says Mr. Big Nose. "What are you two clowns doing here? You're supposed to be writing a book!"

"We are," I say. "At least, we *were*, but we got to page 54 and realized that you hadn't called to remind us about the deadline like you usually do, so *we* called *you*. But you weren't there. It looked suspicious, so we decided to investigate and search for clues."

"And the trail of clues led you here?" says Mr. Big Nose.

"Well, not exactly," I say. "We found a caterpillar in your office. We figured it must have seen what happened to you, and we took it to Jill's house so she could talk to it."

"Ah," says Mr. Big Nose, "so *that's* how you found me."

"Well, no," says Terry, "because Jill had pricked her finger on a carrot and fallen asleep for 100 years."

"So I kissed her to wake her up," I say.

"Eeewwww!" says Jill.

"I know what you mean," says Terry. "And it didn't work anyway, because Andy's not a real prince. So then we had to go on a long journey to find an *actual* prince. But the best we could come up with was a *potato* prince."

"Oh, so *that's* why that potato was slobbering all over me," says Jill.

"Yes," I say, "and I'm sorry about that, but at least you're awake now."

"Yeah," says Terry. "And you can talk to the caterpillar and find out what happened to Mr. Big Nose."

"You fools!" shouts Mr. Big Nose. "You don't have to talk to a *caterpillar*! I'll tell you what happened—I was kidnapped by vegetables, that's what!"

"But why?" says Jill. "Why would vegetables *do* such a thing?"

"Because I published Vegetable Patty's book, *Fun with Vegetables*, that's why. Apparently, they're a little upset about it."

"So the book *was* a clue!" says Terry. "I thought so!"

"You thought *everything* was a clue," I say. "Even your own hand!"

"Did not," says Terry.

"Did so," I say.

"Did not."

"Did so *times infinity*!" I say, which wins the argument, but Terry doesn't hear me over the loud crunching and munching sound coming from just outside the dungeon door.

The sound gets louder and louder and then a hole opens up in the door and the caterpillar pokes its head through.

"Yay!" says Terry. "This is the caterpillar we were telling you about. It's come to save us!"

"That's the stupidest thing I've ever heard," says Mr. Big Nose. "How could a caterpillar save us?"

"By eating all the vegetables, of course," says Terry.

"Yeah," I say, "that caterpillar can eat *anything*! So far today it's eaten *one* flying fried-egg car,

"*one* enormous black bird,

"*two* steamrollers,

"*three* rhinoceroses,

"*four* wacky waving inflatable
arm-flailing tube men,

"*five* giant mutant spiders,

"*one* grumpy old
tomato,

"*one* wall of
asparagus spears

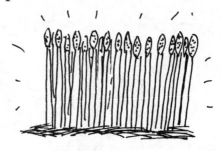

"and *one* reinforced
celery door!"

"That caterpillar is amazing," says Terry. "We should write a book about it."

"Well, don't expect *me* to publish it," says Mr. Big Nose. "As if anyone would want to read a book about a really hungry caterpillar!"

"I would," says Jill. "I love animal stories. But I don't think that caterpillar will be eating anything else today."

"Why not?" says Terry.

"Because it's making a cocoon," says Jill. "And once inside it will transform into a
beautiful butterfly!"

"And *then* will it eat all the vegetables?" says Terry.

"No," says Jill, "because it won't have a mouth . . . just a proboscis for sucking nectar from flowers."

"Well, that's no use to us!" I say. "What are we going to do?!"

"You're going to come with us," says a gruff voice, as two eggplant guards unlock the door and enter the dungeon. "It's lunch time!"

"Oh, thank goodness," says Terry. "I'm starving! What are we having?"

"You soup," says one of the eggplants.

"Mmm," says Terry, "that sounds interesting. What's in it?"

"You!" says the eggplant, pointing at him. Then it turns to the rest of us.

"And you . . .

and you . . .

and you!"

CHAPTER 9

HUMAN SOUP

"Well, this is another fine mess you've gotten us all into, Terry," I say, as we sit in a pot of water suspended over a fire surrounded by a mob of angry vegetables.

"It's not *my* fault," says Terry. "It was *your* idea to come to this stupid castle."

"Only because Jill pricked her finger on a carrot," I say. "If it's anybody's fault, it's Jill's."

"That's got nothing to do with it!" says Jill. "It's obviously Mr. Big Nose's fault for upsetting the vegetables by publishing that mean book."

"It's not *my* fault," says Mr. Big Nose. "It's Vegetable Patty's fault for writing it!"

"Yes, it's Vegetable Patty's fault," I say to the eggplants. "You should catch *her* and put her in the pot and let us all go free. We *love* vegetables!"

"Yes, vegetables are the best!" says Terry. "Long live vegetables!"

"Who are you trying to fool?" says one of the eggplants. "I've read your books! You and Andy *hate* vegetables!"

"No, we don't," I say. "It's fruit we hate—we've got a whole room in our treehouse just for smashing watermelons!"

"Yes, but you also have a vegetable vaporizer," says the eggplant.

"That was *Andy's* idea," says Terry.

"And what about the rocket-powered carrot-launcher?" says the eggplant. "Whose idea was that?"

"Well," says Terry, "that was mine, but the carrots enjoy it!"

"No, they don't! And flying beetroots don't like people riding on them, either. That's why we set them free."

"So that's where our flying beetroots went!" I say.

"Another mystery solved!" says Terry.

"Excuse me," says Jill to the eggplant, "I don't hate vegetables and I'd never *dream* of hurting one so could you let me go, please?"

"No way!" snaps the eggplant. "You feed truckloads of poor defenseless vegetables to your animals every day. That's why we sent that cursed carrot to your house to put you to sleep."

"So *that's* why Jill was asleep!" I say. "She wasn't cursed—the carrot was!"

"Another mystery solved!" says Terry. "We are GREAT detectives. We have solved every mystery that we had today!"

ALL THE MYSTERIES
WE HAVE SOLVED TODAY!

1. The Mystery of ~~CASE CLOSED~~ing Mr. ~~ose~~

2. The Mystery of the Missing ~~CASE CLOSED~~ers

3. The Mystery of Why Everything ~~CASE CLOSED~~erry

4. The Mystery of ~~CASE CLOSED~~ Haven't ~~Lately~~

5. The Mystery of ~~CASE CLOSED~~ll Has a ~~se on Her~~

"Enough jibber-jabber!" says the prince, stepping forward. "You are *all* guilty of anti-vegetable activity and for this you will pay the ultimate price!"

"*A million dollars?!*" says Terry.

"No, you fool," says the prince, "you will pay with your *lives!*"

He turns to face the assembled vegetables. "My loyal subjects," he says, "today we feast . . . on *human soup!*"

The vegetables all start dancing around the pot and chanting.

We've got you in a pot!
And it's starting to get hot!
Do you like it in our pot?
No, we bet that you do not!

225

"Well, it doesn't look like there's much hope for us now," I say. "And to think that it had to happen *today* of *all* possible days."

"What do you mean, Andy?" says Terry.

"You *still* don't remember, do you?!" I say.

"Remember what?" he says.

"Forget it," I say.

"How can I forget it if I can't even remember it in the first place?" says Terry.

"Be quiet, you two," says Mr. Big Nose. "Look at the vegetables! They're slowing down and falling asleep. They appear to have tired themselves out."

"Yay!" says Terry. "We won!"

"Not really," says Mr. Big Nose. "I think you'll find we're still tied up in a pot of water that is getting hotter by the minute."

"Yeah, good point," says Terry. "I guess we lost after all."

Suddenly a ferocious, vegetable-fighting warrior comes flying through the air holding a potato masher in one hand and a vegetable peeler in the other.

"Never fear!"* she says. "Vegetable Patty is here!"

*Unless, of course, you're a vegetable, in which case you *should* fear . . .

quite a lot, actually, because—look out—Vegetable Patty's here!

CHAPTER 10

VEGETABLE PATTY TO THE RESCUE

"Yay!" says Terry. "I knew Vegetable Patty would come to save us! I *knew* everything would be all right."

"I wouldn't be too sure about that," I say. "Look!
The vegetables are waking up, and there's a lot
more of them than there are of her."

"He's right, you know," sneers the prince. "You'll never take us alive!"

"I have no intention of taking you—or any other vegetable here—alive," says Vegetable Patty. "Prepare to be sliced, diced, packed into plastic snap-lock sacks and snap-frozen in my portable freezer!"

She slices!

She dices!

She chops and lops and bops!

She crashes!

She mashes!

She cuts off carrot tops!

She punches!

She crunches!

She grabs and jabs and stabs!

She chomps!

She whomps!

She makes vegetable kebabs!

She kicks!

She flicks!

She whacks and cracks and smacks!

She crushes!

She mushes!

She stuffs them into sacks!*

*Handy resealable plastic snap-lock sacks, which are an ideal size for portable freezers.

Vegetable Patty puts the last of her resealable bags into her freezer and releases us from the pot of near-boiling water.

"Thank you for coming to my rescue, VP," says Mr. Big Nose. "It's *so* good to have an author I can rely on . . . not like these two clowns."

"That's not very nice," says Jill. "Andy and Terry did their best."

"Well, their best wasn't good enough!" says Mr. Big Nose. "But then Patty is a vegetable-fighter, I suppose. *And* a revenge-atarian."

"A *revenge*-atarian?" says Terry. "What's that? Is it like a *vegetarian*?"

"Sort of," says Patty. "I mainly eat vegetables, but it's not because I like them—it's to get revenge on them for the misery they caused me as a child."

"Tell me about it!" I say. "My parents used to make me eat vegetables all the time! It was awful."

"At least you only had to *eat* them," says Terry. "My parents made me *drink* them—vegetable smoothies *three times a day*."

"That's not what I meant," says Vegetable Patty. "I don't hate vegetables because I had to eat them. I hate them because they killed my parents."

"Vegetables *killed* your parents?" says Jill. "But how?"

"It was like this," says Vegetable Patty, taking a deep breath. "One day, when I was quite young, my parents took me to a country fair. We were admiring a display of giant, overgrown vegetables . . .

"when, suddenly, a freak storm hit and a strong gust of wind blew all the enormous vegetables loose from their moorings. They rolled off the stage . . .

Wind ♪

"and squashed both my parents as flat as pancakes."

"I vowed then and there to get revenge by devoting my life to killing and eating as many vegetables as possible!"

"But vegetables taste *horrible*," I say.

"That's true, they do," says Patty, "but the taste of revenge is sweet. They kind of cancel each other out."

"That's why I need you and your readers to help me in my crusade against vegetables by eating as many as you can. The faster we eat them, the sooner we'll wipe them from the face of the earth forever!"

Terry turns to me and whispers, "I hate vegetables as much as anyone, but I don't hate them *that* much."

"Me neither," I say.

Vegetable Patty's phone rings. "What's that?" she says. "Your children are refusing to eat their vegetables? Don't worry . . . I'll be right there!"

She turns to Mr. Big Nose and says, "I have to go. It's an emergency."

"Any chance I could get a lift back to the office?" says Mr. Big Nose. "I'm a busy man, you know, and this whole vegetable-kidnap situation has really put me behind schedule."

"Sure," says Vegetable Patty. "My vegetable-powered revenge-mobile is parked right outside. But there's only room for one passenger."

"That's okay," says Mr. Big Nose, waving his arm dismissively at us. "They can find their own way home."

"Well," I say, "our work here appears to be done. Let's go."

"Remember, it's your turn to be the horse," says Terry.

"Let's not bother with the horse," I say. "Let's take the tram instead."

"There's a *tram*?!" says Terry. "How come we didn't take it to get here?"

"Because you were a horse," I say. "And horses—as everyone knows—are not allowed on trams."

The tram arrives and, even though it's a bit crowded, we manage to find a seat.

"All aboard," says the conductor.
And off we go.

CHAPTER 11

SURPRISE!

It's quite a long trip home.

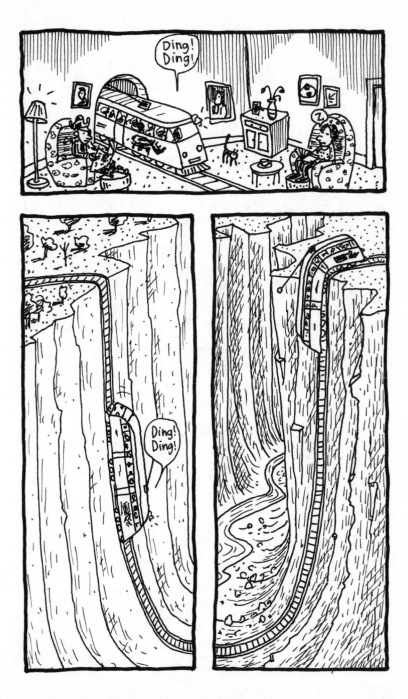

Finally, we arrive at Jill's stop.
   She gets off and we wave good-bye.

The next stop is ours.

We get off the tram and climb up to our treehouse.

It's great to be home again, but there is a lot to do.
There are sharks to feed . . .

watermelons to smash . . .

waves to surf . . .

chainsaws to juggle . . .

rocking horses to race . . .

and make-your-own pizzas don't make
themselves, you know.

"So," says Terry, as we float around in our see-through swimming pool, "that all worked out pretty well!"

"Yeah, except for one thing," I say.

"What?" says Terry.

"Except that today is my *birthday* and you *completely forgot* about it!"

"Today is your birthday?!" says Terry. "You should have told me!"

"I just *did*," I say, "but I shouldn't have had to! You should have remembered. That's what friends do!"

"I'm sorry," says Terry. "But before I met you I'd never had a friend, and I've *never* had a birthday, so I didn't know."

"You've never had a birthday?" I say. "Why not?"

"My parents thought they were too dangerous," says Terry.

ALL THE THINGS THAT MAKE BIRTHDAYS DANGEROUS (ACCORDING TO TERRY'S PARENTS)

SIGN COULD FALL AND CATCH FIRE OR CHOKE SOMEONE OR BOTH

LETTER "P" COULD DROP OFF AND BREAK SOMEONE'S BRAIN

RISK OF HYPERVENTILATION OR DIZZINESS FROM TRYING TO BLOW OUT EVERY LAST BIRTHDAY CANDLE

CHILD COULD SUCK INSTEAD OF BLOW AND SWALLOW FLAME

CHILD LEANING FORWARD ON CHAIR

SHARP CAKE-CUTTING KNIFE

DANGEROUS REPTILE LEFT UNDER TABLE

"So when *is* your birthday?" I say.

"I don't know," says Terry. "We never celebrated it so I'm not sure when it is."

I think for a moment.

There's only one thing to do.

"Terry?" I say.

"Yes?"

"You can share my birthday."

"Really?"

"Yes, and because I never forget my own birthday, I'll never forget yours either, so I'll be able to remind you. We'll celebrate together every year . . . starting today."

"Thanks, Andy," says Terry. "You're the best friend I've ever had. Just one question."

"What's that?"

"How old are we?"

"It's funny you should ask," I say, "because that's what I was about to tell the readers at the start of the book."

"And what's the answer?"

"Well," I say, "we are—"

"Andy!" calls a voice from the forest. "Terry! Come quick!"

"That's Jill!" I say.

"And it sounds like she's in trouble," says Terry.

"I hope it's not more *vegetable* trouble!" I say. "Come on! Let's go!"

We each grab a vine, swing to the bottom of the
tree and rush into the forest.

"Jill!" I call. "Where are you?"
"I'm over here!" she says. "Hurry!"
"Don't worry, we're coming!" says Terry.

We run into a clearing.
"SURPRISE!" yells Jill.

CHAPTER 12

A CRAZY PLAN

"Happy Birthday, Andy!" says Jill.

"Thanks, Jill," I say. "But can this be Terry's party too because today is his birthday as well?"

"I didn't know it was *your* birthday, Terry," says Jill. "Andy's been dropping hints for months, but you never said a word."

"That's because my parents never told me when my birthday was," says Terry, "so I didn't know. But Andy said I could share his."

"That's so nice of you, Andy!" says Jill. "Happy Birthday, Terry. I'll just get Mr. Hee-Haw to add your name to the birthday banner."

"Jill," I say, "this is amazing, but how did you organize it all so quickly? I mean, we only got back from the vegetable castle a couple of hours ago!"

"The animals and I have been planning your surprise party for weeks," says Jill. "It was while we were getting everything ready that I pricked my finger on that cursed carrot. But, luckily, when I woke up, the animals did too and they finished getting the party ready while I was away. They really love a party . . . as you can see."

"Look!" says Terry. "A butterfly. And it says HAPPY BIRTHDAY on its wings!"

"That's because it's a *birthday* butterfly!" says Jill.

"Why is it wearing the caterpillar's hat?" says Terry.

"Because it used to *be* the caterpillar," says Jill.

"Huh?" says Terry. "How could a caterpillar turn into a butterfly?"

"Metamorphosis," says Jill.

"What's that?" says Terry.

"I'll explain later," I say.

"Birthdays are really fun!" says Terry, his face covered in Edward Scooperhand's birthday cake–flavored ice-cream cake. "I think we should have one every day!"

BEAM
BEAM

"But that's not how birthdays work," I say. "You only get one per year because, otherwise, you would get too old too fast."

"Hey, I know," says Terry. "Why don't we make a birthday level in our treehouse where it can be your birthday whenever you want but you don't get any older?"

"I think you might be on to something!" I say.

"Hmmm, that's weird," says Terry. "It sounds like our 3-D video phone, but it can't be, because what would it be doing down here in the forest?"

"Actually, it *is* your 3-D video phone," says Jill. "I had Larry, Curly and Moe bring it down here in case Mr. Big Nose rang to wish you Happy Birthday. That's probably him now. You'd better answer it."

"Hello, Andy and Terry," says Mr. Big Nose. "I guess you know why I'm calling."

"To wish us a Happy Birthday?" I say.

"Don't be ridiculous!" says Mr. Big Nose. "I'm calling to tell you your book is due at five o'clock."

"Five o'clock tomorrow?" says Terry.

"No, five o'clock today!" says Mr. Big Nose.

"But we're not finished," I say. "We've been too busy rescuing you!"

"That's not my problem," says Mr. Big Nose. "A contract is a contract! That book had better be here by five . . . OR ELSE!"

He hangs up.

I look at Terry.

Terry looks at me.

"I think it's time for presents," says Jill, handing us a parcel wrapped in gold paper with a big purple bow.

"But how can we open presents at a time like this?" I say. "If we don't get our book written then . . . then . . . then I don't know what will happen, but it will probably involve Mr. Big Nose getting so mad that his nose explodes and us having to go back to work at the monkey house."

"Don't worry," says Jill, "just trust me. Open your present. I think you'll like it."

We unwrap the parcel.

"It's a book!" I say.

"I *love* books!" says Terry. "What is it called?"

"*The 52-Story Treehouse!*"

"I *love* that book!" says Terry.

"No you don't," I say, "I mean, you can't . . . because we haven't even written it yet!"

"No," says Jill, "*you* haven't . . . but *I* have—all the words *and* the pictures."

"But how?" I say.

"With the help of my animals, of course," says Jill. "You might not think it to look at them, but they're really quite talented. And it was the least I could do after you and Terry went to so much trouble to rescue me from my enchanted sleep."

"Can we read it now?" says Terry.

"Of course!" says Jill.

We read the book . . .

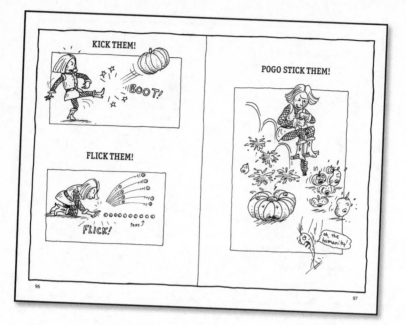

"GREAT idea," I say. "And since you thought of it, you can go first."

"Thanks, Andy!" says Terry, taking the costume. "You're a real pal."

He puts it on and we set off.

"What a lovely day for horse-riding," I say.

"Is it your turn to be the horse yet?" says Terry.

"No, not yet," I say.

"How's the caterpillar?" says Terry.

"Good," I say. "I think it's really enjoying the ride."

"I sure hope we don't come across anything that would be hazardous to caterpillars on our journey," says Terry.

"That must be him! That's Prince Potato!" says Terry, pointing to a large potato wearing a small golden crown. "But he's not very handsome."

"No," I say. "He's pretty good-looking for a potato though."

"Oh, my!" says the prince, stopping next to us. "Do my ten eyes deceive or is this a princess in a glass coffin I see before me?"

"No," says Terry, "Jill's not a—"

I stamp on Terry's foot to shut him up.

"Yes, Your Highness!" I say quickly. "She is indeed a princess but she is under a terrible spell and only the kiss of a handsome prince will wake her."

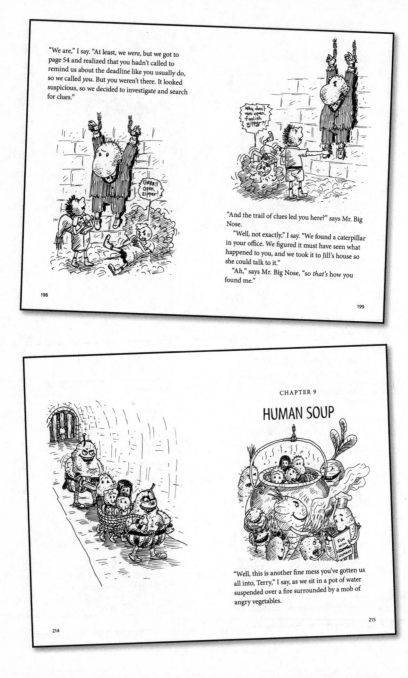

"We are," I say. "At least, we *were*, but we got to page 54 and realized that you hadn't called to remind us about the deadline like you usually do, so *we* called *you*. But you weren't there. It looked suspicious, so we decided to investigate and search for clues."

"And the trail of clues led you here?" says Mr. Big Nose.

"Well, not exactly," I say. "We found a caterpillar in your office. We figured it must have seen what happened to you, and we took it to Jill's house so she could talk to it."

"Ah," says Mr. Big Nose, "so *that's* how you found me."

CHAPTER 9

HUMAN SOUP

"Well, this is another fine mess you've gotten us all into, Terry," I say, as we sit in a pot of water suspended over a fire surrounded by a mob of angry vegetables.

"That's why I need you and your readers to help me in my crusade against vegetables by eating as many as you can. The faster we eat them, the sooner we'll wipe them from the face of the earth forever!"

Terry turns to me and whispers, "I hate vegetables as much as anyone, but I don't hate them *that* much."

"Me neither," I say.

Vegetable Patty's phone rings. "What's that?" she says. "Your children are refusing to eat their vegetables? Don't worry . . . I'll be right there!"

She turns to Mr. Big Nose and says, "I have to go. It's an emergency."

CHAPTER 12

A CRAZY PLAN

"Well," says Jill, "what do you think?"

"Action-packed!" I say. "I love it! But how will we get it to Mr. Big Nose in time?"

"What about the birthday butterfly?" says Terry.

"No," says Jill, "the book would be too heavy for it to carry. Butterflies are beautiful, but they are not very strong."

299

298

"Well," says Jill, "what do you think?"

"Action-packed!" I say. "I love it! But how will we get it to Mr. Big Nose in time?"

"What about the birthday butterfly?" says Terry.

"No," says Jill, "the book would be too heavy for it to carry. Butterflies are beautiful, but they are not very strong."

"What about Silky and the other flying cats?" I say. "Could they take it?"

"I'm afraid not," says Jill, "they're on holiday in the Catnary Islands. I got this postcard from them yesterday."

CATNARY ISLANDS ©

Dear Jill,
having a nice time. So far
we've been fishing, bird-
watching, bird-catching,
bird-eating and
parasailing.
lots of love
Silky and the gang

To Jill
Jill's house
Near the forest
World

"I know," says Terry. "We can use the cannon!"

"No you can't," says Jill. "A robin built her nest in it and the baby birds have just hatched. They must not be disturbed."

"Then I guess we're doomed," says Terry. "Unless . . ."

Jill and I lean forward.

"Unless what?" I say.

"Unless we get my Ninja Snails to deliver it."

"But that will take *forever*!" I say.

"Not forever," says Terry. "Only about 100 years and 15 minutes by my calculations."

"Great," I say, "except that it will be 100 years too late for Mr. Big Nose."

"No it won't," says Terry. "Not if we *stop time*."

"Well, duh," I say, "as if we could do that."

"I think we could," says Terry. "I've still got the carrot that Jill pricked her finger on. I collected it as evidence when we were trying to solve *The Mystery of Why Jill Has a Curse on Her*."

"But how is a cursed carrot going to help us stop time?" I say.

"Like this!" says Terry. "We use the rocket-powered carrot-launcher to fire the carrot into the heart of the Greenwich Observatory—which is where all the time in the world comes from. If you stop time there, you stop time everywhere, which will give the Ninja Snails all the time they need."

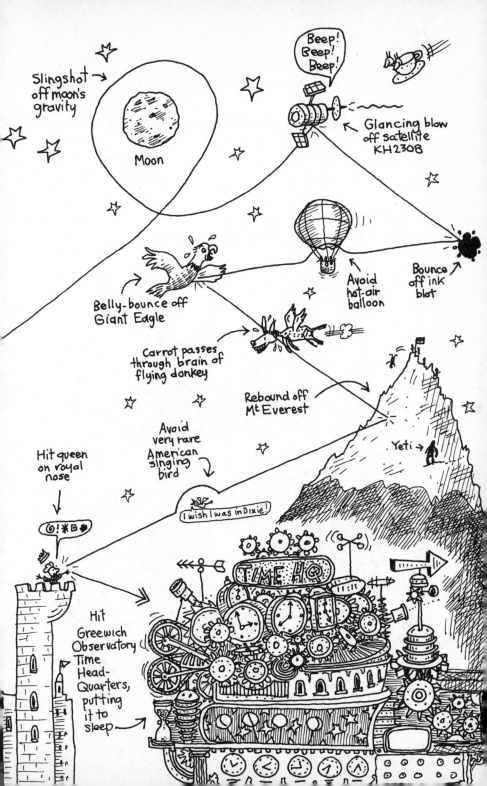

"But what about the snails?" I say. "Won't it put *them* to sleep too?"

"No," says Terry, "because they're *Ninja* Snails. The normal laws of time and space don't apply to them."

"That's crazy, Terry," I say.

"Oh." He sighs in disappointment.

"*So* crazy it might just work!"

"Great!" says Terry. "To the treehouse!"

Jill and I follow Terry to the treehouse and climb up to the Ninja Snail Training Academy. Terry explains the mission to the snails, gives them the book and fires a starting pistol.

He waves good-bye to the snails.

"Good luck," he says. "Don't forget to send me a telegram when you arrive."

He turns to us. "Now let's go launch that carrot."

Terry loads the carrot into the carrot-launcher and points it in the direction of Greenwich Observatory.

"Here goes," he says, pushing the launch button.

The carrot shoots into the sky and disappears into the clouds.

"Well," says Terry, "the carrot is on its way. We'd better go to the room full of pillows and get comfortable. We've got a long sleep ahead of us."

"Do you really think Terry's plan will work?" says Jill as she snuggles into a pile of pillows.

"I hope so," I say. "Are you feeling tired yet?"

Jill yawns. "Maybe a little bit," she says.

"Yeah," I say, yawning. "Me too. What about you, Terry?"

He doesn't answer.

"Terry?" I say. I look over. Terry is snoring.

"He's asleep," I say to Jill.

But Jill doesn't hear me. She's asleep too.

Which just leaves me. I'm the only one who's not aslee . . . zzzzzzzzzzzzzzzzzzzzzzzzzzzzzzzzzz
zzzzzzzzzzzzzzzzzzzzzzzzzzzzzzzzzzzzzzzzzzzz
zzzzzzzzzzzzzzzzzzzzzzzzzzzzzzzzzzzzzzzzzzzz
zzzzzzzzzzzzzzzzzzzzzzzzzzzzzzzzzzzzzzzzzzzz
zzzzzzzzzzzzzzzzzzzzzzzzzzzzzzzzzzzzzzzzzzzz
zzzzzzzzzzzzzzzzzzzzzzzzzzzzzzzzzzzzzzzzzzzz
zzzzzzzzzzzzzzzzzzzzzzzzzzzzzzzzzzzzzzzzzzzz
zzzzzzzzzzzzzzzzzzzzzzzzzzzzzzzzzzzzzzzzzzzz
zzzzzzzzzzzzzzzzzzzzzzzzzzzzzzzzzzzzzzzzzzzz
zzzzzzzzzzzzzzzzzzzzzzzzzzzzzzzzzzzzzzzzzzzz
zzzzzzzzzzzzzzzzzzzzzzzzzzzzzzzzzzzzzzzzzzzz
zzzzzzzzzzzzzzzzzzzzzzzzzzzzzzzzzzzzzzzzzzzz
zzzzzzzzzzzzzzzzzzzzzzzzzzzzzzzzzzzzzzzzzzzz
zzzzzzzzzzzzzzzzzzzzzzzzzzzzzzzzzzzzzzzzzzzz

ZZZZZZZZZZZZZZZZZZZZZZZZZZZZZZZZZZZZZZZZZZZZZZZZZZ
ZZZZZZZZZZZZZZZZZZZZZZZZZZZZZZZZZZZZZZZZZZZZZZZZZZ
ZZZZZZZZZZZZZZZZZZZZZZZZZZZZZZZZZZZZZZZZZZZZZZZZZZ
ZZZZZZZZZZZZZZZZZZZZZZZZZZZZZZZZZZZZZZZZZZZZZZZZZZ
ZZZZZZZZZZZZZZZZZZZZZZZZZZZZZZZZZZZZZZZZZZZZZZZZZZ
ZZZZZZZZZZZZZZZZZZZZZZZZZZZZZZZZZZZZZZZZZZZZZZZZZZ
ZZZZZZZZZZZZZZZZZZZZZZZZZZZZZZZZZZZZZZZZZZZZZZZZZZ
ZZZZZZZZZZZZZZZZZZZZZZZZZZZZZZZZZZZZZZZZZZZZZZZZZZ
ZZZZZZZZZZZZZZZZZZZZZZZZZZZZZZZZZZZZZZZZZZZZZZZZZZ
ZZZZZZZZZZZZZZZZZZZZZZZZZZZZZZZZZZZZZZZZZZZZZZZZZZ
ZZZZZZZZZZZZZZZZZZZZZZZZZZZZZZZZZZZZZZZZZZZZZZZZZZ
ZZZZZZZZZZZZZZZZZZZZZZZZZZZZZZZZZZZZZZZZZZZZZZZZZZ
ZZZZZZZZZZZZZZZZZZZZZZZZZZZZZZZZZZZZZZZZZZZZZZZZZZ
ZZZZZZZZZZZZZZZZZZZZZZZZZZZZZZZZZZZZZZZZZZZZZZZZZZ
ZZZZZZZZZZZZZZZZZZZZZZZZZZZZZZZZZZZZZZZZZZZZZZZZZZ
ZZZZZZZZZZZZZZZZZZZZZZZZZZZZZZZZZZZZZZZZZZZZZZZZZZ
ZZZZZZZZZZZZZZZZZZZZZZZZZZZZZZZZZZZZZZZZZZZZZZZZZZ
ZZZZZZZZZZZZZZZZZZZZZZZZZZZZZZZZZZZZZZZZZZZZZZZZZZ
ZZZZZZZZZZZZZZZZZZZZZZZZZZZZZZZZZZZZZZZZZZZZZZZZZZ
ZZZZZZZZZZZZZZZZZZZZZZZZZZZZZZZZZZZZZZZZZZZZZZZZZZ
ZZZZZZZZZZZZZZZZZZZZZZZZZZZZZZZZZZZZZZZZZZZZZZZZZZ
ZZZZZZZZZZZZZZZZZZZZZZZZZZZZZZZZZZZZZZZZZZZZZZZZZZ
ZZZZZZZZZZZZZZZZZZZZZZZZZZZZZZZZZZZZZZZZZZZZZZZZZZ
ZZZZZZZZZZZZZZZZZZZZZZZZZZZZZZZZZZZZZZZZZZZZZZZZZ . . .

CHAPTER 13

THE LAST CHAPTER

THE BALLAD OF
THE NINJA SNAILS

It was a group of Ninja Snails,
All schooled in an ancient art,
That set out one day on an epic trip,
Prepared to play their part.

Their precious cargo—a silly book—

They had to deliver on time

To Mr. Big Nose, the publisher,
Before five o'clock did'st chime.

O'er hill and dale the snails did slide

Though they grew pale and wan;

They were weak and tired and in need of rest,
But still the snails slid on.

Would they make it? Could they take it?

The conclusion was not foregone.

The odds were against them.
(Fate seemed to hate them!)
But still the snails slid on.

As the years did pass, the landscape changed

That the snails were sliming upon:

Seeds became trees and forests grew,
But still the snails slid on.

The ice did melt and the seas did rise;

The low-lying land was all gone.

The climate warmed—a new world formed,
But still the snails slid on.

They were desperate to arrive at the office by five,

But time marched never on.

They wished to end their epic quest,
But still the snails slid on . . . and on . . . and on . . .
and on . . . and on . . . and on . . . and on . . . and on . . .

Till, finally, they saw a sign—
A nose so big and red—
Their journey's end was reached at last,
And up the walls they "sped."

They reached the open office window
And slowly slid inside.
They slimed onto the office desk
And across it they did glide.

So let's hear it for those snails so brave,
Let's give them three big cheers,
For they made their way and saved the day
(Though it took 100 years*).

---

* And 15 minutes.

. . . ZZZZZZZZZZZZZZZZZZZZZZZZZZZZZZZZZZZZZZZZZZZZZZZ
ZZZZZZZZZZZZZZZZZZZZZZZZZZZZZZ

ZZZZZZZZZZZZ . . . um . . . hang on . . . what are these zees doing all over the page?

Oh . . . I must have fallen asleep.

I wonder what the time is?

I look at the clock.

Hang on! That can't be right! It's fast—*100 years and 15 minutes fast!*

Ah!

Now I remember.

The carrot!

The Ninja Snails!

The book!

Terry's crazy plan!

"Terry!" I say. "Jill! Wake up!"

Terry sits up and rubs his eyes.

Jill yawns and stretches. "I feel like I've been asleep for 100 years and 15 minutes," she says.

"That's because you *have*!" I say. "We *all* have."

"I wonder if the snails made it?" says Terry.

At that moment the doorbell rings.

We go down and open the door.

It's Bill the postman!

"Gee, you guys have really let this place go," says Bill. "I had to clear a path to get in here! I'm a postman, not a gardener, you know."

"Sorry, Bill," I say. "We slept in."

"For 100 years and 15 minutes," says Terry.

"You boys need an alarm clock," says Bill, chuckling.

"I hate alarms," says Terry. "They scare me."

"How do you feel about telegrams?" says Bill.

"I *love* them!" says Terry.

"Well, that's great," says Bill, "because I've got one for you right here."

"Yay!" says Terry, taking the telegram from Bill. "It's from the snails!"

"What does it say?" says Jill.

"They made it!"

Snail nibbles

TELEGRAM

RECEIVER : TERRY   SENDER : NINJA SNAILS

GREETINGS, MASTER TERRY.

BOOK DELIVERED.
ON OUR WAY BACK.
SEE YOU IN 100 YEARS (AND 15 MINUTES).

LOVE FROM THE NINJA SNAILS.

"That's wonderful news," says Jill.

"Yeah," says Terry. "I *knew* they could do it."

"Me too," I say. "I'm going to miss those little guys."

"Not for long," says Terry. "They're on their way home!"

"Always glad to be the bearer of good news," says Bill, "but I'd better be on my way." He rides his scooter back down the path he's cleared to our front door and disappears into the overgrown forest.

"I had the most amazing dream while we were asleep," says Terry. "I dreamed we added another 13 stories to the treehouse, including one where it's always your birthday."

"Me too!" I say, "I had the *exact same dream*!"

"So did *I*," says Jill, "and one of the new stories was a pet-grooming salon—and I was in charge!"

"It's kind of weird that we all had the same dream," says Terry. "Do you think it means something?"

"Definitely," I say. "It means we should add another 13 stories to the treehouse and we should get started right away."

"Don't forget the pet-grooming salon," says Jill.

"Or the birthday room," says Terry.

"One 65-story treehouse with a pet-grooming salon and a birthday room coming right up!" I say.

THE END

Andy Griffiths lives in a 52-story treehouse with his friend Terry and together they make funny books, just like the one you're holding in your hands right now. Andy writes the words and Terry draws the pictures. If you'd like to know more, read this book (or visit www.andygriffiths.com.au).

Terry Denton lives in a 52-story treehouse with his friend Andy and together they make funny books, just like the one you're holding in your hands right now. Terry draws the pictures and Andy writes the words. If you'd like to know more, read this book (or visit www.terrydenton.com).

Get ready for more
LAUGH ATTACKS
from Andy Griffiths and Terry Denton!